Scarecrow, Where Do You Go?

starring Patch

Written by Andy Z
With illustrations by Woody Miller

Scarecrow, scarecrow

out in the field.
He's made of straw and
you know he's not real.

But the crow's won't come near,
now that doesn't seem right.

Just you wait, 'til the stroke of
midnight!

He moves one arm . . .

He moves the other arm . . .

He moves one leg . . .

He moves the other leg . . .

He shakes his head all around,

and he wiggles his toes.

Then it's 1 - 2 - 3 and . . .

Away he goes!

Scarecrow, scarecrow
running so fast!

Scarecrow **running**

forward and back ...

He runs to the left!

He runs to the right!

He runs and runs
'til he sees **daylight!**

Then it's back to
the field, because
he knows...

cock-a-doodle-doo!

He'll move no more when
the rooster crows!

Scarecrow
scarecrow

scarecrow
scarecrow

Scarecrow, scarecrow
out in the corn...
Now that doesn't seem right!

Why are your clothes so
tattered and torn,
when you can't
move an inch?

But now we know what you do at

midnight!

You move one arm . . .
you move the other arm . . .

You move one leg . . .

you move the other leg.

You shake your head all around,

and you wiggle your toes.

Then it's 1 - 2 - 3 and . . .

Away you go!

The End

Scarecrow, Where do you go?

For my family, and for the kids and folks whose imaginations and support make adventures in Andyland possible!
- A.Z.

For Jill, where do you go at midnight?
- W.M.

This book is taken from the song "Scarecrow" written and performed by Andy Z
To hear the song and purchase his albums, visit **www.andyz.com**

Website address:
www.andyz.com
www.woodymillerart.com

Made in the USA
Charleston, SC
11 October 2010